Successful Life
Or
Successful Living

Your Choice...

S. Nand

Edited by : Padmini B Patell

Publisher: Notion Press through Self-Publishing Platform

Edited by Padmini B Patell

Designed by Shankar Pulgam

Disclaimer: Author disclaims any implied warranties, merchantability or fitness for error, omission, mistake or discrepancy. However, if brought to notice, it will be taken care of in the next edition. All disputes are subject to Hyderabad jurisdiction only.

Copyright:
All learnings and experiences in this book are from my life, so anyone and everyone can copy or share any contents with friends, relatives, and well-wishers. I have also no objection to any organization publishing and gifting this book to its employees.
The essence of life is sharing, and we have the privilege of sharing only till we are alive.

For any queries/suggestions please contact :
@ S. Nand
Email: snand.csd@gmail.com
Phone No +91-7702222851

This book is a dedication to
Param Pujya Shirdi Sai,
whose blessings have empowered
me to have a life of fulfilment.

ACKNOWLEDGEMENT

I gratefully acknowledge the contribution and guidance from numerous eminent trainers and authors, who enabled me to continue on the path of learning for more than five decades and conduct hundreds of workshops singlehandedly. Significant insights accrued from these interactions with sharing of experiences by thousands of participants, all of which built the foundation of this book.

I feel blessed to have a loving family and friends, who are my pillars of support and were on my side throughout to meet challenges of life successfully.

Finally, I am grateful to the participants of these workshops, whose motivation helped me to share all my thoughts, learnings, and insights in this book form.

When it comes to book getting the shape, it was possible only because of so many efforts put in by editor Ms Padmini Patell. For keying in help from Mr Sudhir Pillai of JPL was rendered. Cover page was conceived by Mr Sunil Masuriha, however Mr Shankar Pulgam did all the designing, artwork and formatting. Guidance in publishing was given by Ms Yamini, Notion Press.. My heartfelt gratitude to all of them.

CONTENTS

PREFACE

For a long time, I have been requested by family, friends and many of my participants to compile and share my thoughts on Successful Living. The project has been on my mind for the last two years; however, it has taken shape in the last few months and this is a dream fulfilled.

My two earlier books in Hindi **"Sakaratmak Soch"** (Positive Thinking) and **"Jeevan ke Rang, Khusiyon ke Sang"** (Living Life Happily) have been in circulation for the last two decades and has received much love from all of you, which is proved by the fact that more than 6000 copies of each have reached readers. These books were gifted by organizations to their participants of my workshops as course material. Although I conducted many workshops in English but only my books in Hindi were made available. This motivated me to pen my thoughts in English.

This book titled, **"Successful Life or Successful Living: Your Choice"** itself suggests understanding the difference between these two choices and then goes on to narrate simple ways through ten success mantras, which are shared by me in my workshops, to live a happy, successful & fulfilled life. The normal perception of achieving success in life is having power, position, money, assets and possessions that give comfort. One could have all these, but if these are acquired at the cost of happiness, health, peace and well-being, the price is too high to pay. Living a Life without a sense of purpose is simply existing and not living. A purposeful life lived with happiness, health & peace makes our stay on this earth worthwhile.

All around the world technology has impacted life. Mobile phones are not only being used by rich people, but even by daily wage earners too. Covid made education reach beyond the four walls of school and online education is being widely utilised. Have myself operating on Zoom with help from my grandchildren in those times and since then conducting my workshops online.

Lifestyle has improved, yet life is stressful and mechanical, relationships strained, human connections missing, and Success is being achieved at the cost of living life itself. We need to pause and reflect at our paradigms, beliefs, ways of spending our time and choice of responses. Many such questions were in my mind when I started working for myself after more than three decades of corporate learning. While seeking answers to these, I discovered new and innovative always existed, but their presence was not acknowledged by all, as we looked for very complex ways to move forward. On the contrary, to my surprise, the answers were very easy, simple and useful.

My mission statement was coined in 2001, when I left working for corporate's and started working for myself. It was, **"To assist people and organizations assist in attaining their potential"** and this has remained my guiding force since, in all my projects and endeavours. Little did I realise, that this journey will shape my own beliefs, paradigms, my passion and my life itself and take me to unknown but interesting realms of learning. My journey itself started as a Trainer but took me to new roles of Coach, Mentor, People Process Facilitator, OD Practitioner and Motivational speaker in the last two decades. Learning was my hobby right from childhood, I pursued it in the corporate world and converted it into a passion while interacting with more than two lakh participants of all ages, in all roles and innumerable organizations. The interfaces made me learn so much, gave me new insights by the experiences shared and exchange of ideas. Interestingly, common to all, was that everyone had a life, everyone wanted happiness, everyone had challenges, everyone had success stories to share, and everyone wanted success. However, sadly a number of these were living a routine, mundane and stressful life. The day started with waking up in the morning and ended with sleeping at night and the day passing without any significant happy experience or a sense of joy, and this continued every day, for years.

This made me reflect on whether a meaningful joyful life can be lived by a normal person, while carrying out daily responsibilities and made the way for sharing of my thoughts based on learning from my own life. The journey was initiated about 25 years back at Indore with interactions on positive thinking, which helped me significantly to carry out my responsibilities and for choosing effective responses to umpteen number of challenges, small and big. Luckily, the opportunity to conduct these workshops at the Indore Management Association(IMA) sharpened my own skills, motivated me, made me learn so much from interactions at IMA, where hundreds of participants joined from almost all the organizations. The feedback that participants, who attended my workshops, showed more positive attitude at work, was highly motivating. The experience, however, impacted my own life so much that I finally decided to start working for myself in 2001.

Looking back, I realise the reason of great success of these workshops was that for many decades, training was confined to executives and managers and was not extended to frontline shop floor associates, and it was the first initiative through IMA that touched their attitudes, their life and made them realise their significant role in the organization. They responded with great zeal and started practicing on the shop floor, which then transformed the work culture at many organizations. My own experiences of NTPC Shaktinagar, the first Super Thermal Power Plant and then of NTPC Unchahar turnaround reinforced my belief that associates are the most important stakeholders of any organization. This is logical too as organizations are profited by the support of their customers for quantity, quality and on time delivery of products and services – all three are largely impacted by performance and attitude of associates. Fortunately, this became my USP to all organizations, touched by me in the last two decades and remains so.

I instituted the Centre for Self-Development in 2001 and continued conducting workshops always keeping my mission statement in focus. The journey that started with interactions on positive thinking, moved to happiness and finally life. The contents accordingly kept getting extended to include these. Since I believe that any interaction can be effective only if it is simple, interesting, and practicable, the success mantras were developed, which are simple, interesting and if practiced can help in living a happy and meaningful life. The beauty is anyone can practice these irrespective of his age, role, or organization. It is heartening that hundreds are even now in my contact after several years and share stories of their successful living.

All this led to the birth of the book "Successful Life or Successful Living: Your Choice." .The very purpose of this book is to help one realise that it is possible for him/her to practice successful living (a life with happiness, health and energy, enthusiasm, and passion), meet challenges of life and live a meaningful, purposeful life. Let me reiterate knowledge is good, learning is better, but it is only application that gives meaning to knowledge and learning. The application is optional, but application alone can guarantee the outcome.

Lastly, I would like to humbly share that I did not create all these success mantras. These have always existed. I only kept experimenting with life and learned these simple replicable concepts that can pave a beautiful path to Successful Living. Finally, life is made of choices. Many of these are made by others for us but the important ones are those which we make for ourselves. Thus, it is your choice to go through the book, learn the success mantras and practice them for Successful Living. I believe you can, and you will make that choice.

Successful Living
or
Successful Life
Your choice ...

Life is so intriguing, but it can also be so meaningful. However, while fulfilling day-to-day obligations, many of us forget living life itself. The intricacies, the challenges of life take all our attention and life falls into a routine, where every day it is the same morning, same evening, and same night. Life is not a calendar on which every day a date changes, after a month the page changes and after a year the calendar is changed and with a new calendar, the same is repeated. Every day of life is a new day and in fact, it is the first day of the rest of your life. It is an opportunity to try new things, create new vistas and fulfill the day with happiness, love, and healthy spirit.

Living the routine in the same mundane way, life loses its flavor just like stale food after a day or two. We get tired fighting with the challenges and when we look back, we have only regrets. We just keep telling ourselves, 'Wish I had done it' or 'Wish I had not done it'.

The tragedy is life cannot be lived backwards. Soren Kierkegaard has rightly said **"Life can only be understood backwards; but it must be lived forwards."** There is no option to go back and relive a moment that has passed.

We have only two choices of living a moment. Make it a moment of regret or alternatively make it a moment of beautiful memories.

If we decide, we can make such lovely memories every day and then we can live the days ahead with the motivation drawn from such memories.

We all are fully aware that we cannot have a memory in our life without being part of it. This can be easily done by working on our thoughts and actions.

Your life is unique, and only you can decide what to do with it.

"Do not go where the path may lead, go instead where there is no path and leave a trail." -Ralph Waldo Emerson

Let me share a story.

There was a potter man who was making Chilams (smoking pipes of mud). His wife asked him to start making *surahis* (earthen pot to store water, which after storage gets cooled). The potter started making *surahis*. When he almost finished making the first piece, he heard a voice "Dear Potter man, thank you, thank you". The potter was astonished and asked the voice to identify itself. The voice said, "I am the mud with which you made the *surahi*. On being asked by the potter man, why he is being thanked, the mud responded, "When you were making me into chilam, I was burning with fire and people were smoking and spoiling their health, so I thought of myself as unfortunate. Now you are making me into a *surahi* , I remain cool and feel fortunate as people drink cold water from me." The potter man said, "my thinking was changed because of my wife." To which the voice of the mud said, "for you, only your thinking changed but for me, my life changed."

The simple story illustrates how change of our thoughts and actions can transform our life as well as the life of others.

Life is made of choices. There are many, which are made for us by others, such as where we are born, who our parents will be, in which school we will start our education. Yet important ones are those which we make for ourselves such as what we will make of our life, how will we utilize the time given to us, what will be our values and many more.

What we create everyday depends on our actions which depend on our thoughts. We have the power to create beautiful memories for our benefit and for the benefit of others. If it is so simple, why does it not happen? The main reason is we keep our minds closed. Until and unless we keep our minds open, we cannot escape routine, live in a new way, and make living a beautiful pursuit.

In my workshop 'Living Life Happily & Successfully' I share ten success mantras, which are very simple and can be practiced very easily by anyone and everyone. Also, it has been clearly established by participants, who tried to apply these in their life, that the application has resulted in increased happiness and helped them meet challenges of life successfully.

Interestingly, my interactions varied from teenagers to students of Engineering & Management. From corporate to government departments and Senior citizens. From ward boys/nurses to senior doctors and Deans of medical colleges & from schoolteachers to Directors of large companies. The same Success Mantras were shared except for the language and the examples shared were made relevant to the target audience. Looking back, I find that all the participants exhibited interest, shared their experiences, validating the learning's and not only gave encouraging feedback but even applied many of these success mantras in their life after the workshops, a fact brought out while revisiting them. All this has validated the authenticity of these concepts over the last two decades. The Success Mantras are simple, easy to understand and apply. They do not require position, power, money, or assets to get benefits by their application. This is because everyone has a life and has the power to make choices to live it the way he desires. These simple choices then can result into actions, which can get the desired outcome. Right Choices, Right Actions and Right

Outcome, all go together. These facts validated the Success Mantras and encouraged me to compile these into a book.

SAMWAAD (interactive way) is utilized by me to share these in my workshops. I understand that *SAMWAAD* is effective only if it is simple, interesting, and practical and I have tried to follow these myself utilizing relevant stories, songs and videos in my workshops.

In the pages that follow, each success mantra will be explained and the simple way to apply it, with the hope that it will help anyone going through the book to live a happier, successful, and

1

Waking Up
HAPPILY
In the Morning

Waking up Happily in the Morning

Success Mantra - 1
Waking Up **HAPPILY** *In the Morning*

Let us start by trying to find a response to the question: What is Life? There are many ways by which it is defined by people, but a simple and universally true definition is, **"Life is the time span between birth and death."** There is only limited time at our disposal. Therefore, when we waste time, we waste life. This must make us realize the value and worth of every moment. Money, we lose can be regained, but this is not true for time. Every moment we get only once in our life, and we cannot go back and do anything in the moment that has passed.

This brings us to an interesting fact – the hard truth of life. Neither birth nor death is in our control. Then what is that which is in our control? It is how we utilize every moment, what we do in the moment. We choose what we do, and these choices make our life.

A philosopher was asked **"What is the meaning of Life?"** The Philosopher replied, **"There is no meaning of life, it is an opportunity to create a meaningful life."**

Accepting life is time and time is life, we can now agree that time is quantitative such as seconds, minutes, hours, days, years & decades. The practical unit of time is a day, and each day is divided into morning, evening, and night. The day starts in the morning. Every day is the first day of the rest of life, therefore every morning is the first of the remaining mornings available to us.

The question I ask is, "Why do we do anything in life? To get what?

Money, Car, Bungalow, Position, Prestige, love etc. etc. Yes?

Then the next question I ask is, "what do we get when we get all these? And the simple answer that comes from one and all is "Happiness". True, the ultimate objective of life is to be happy. We do everything so that we can get happiness. For understanding what happiness is, we will wait for the moment as it is complex and critical. My next question is "What is easier - saying a thing or doing it?" Obviously, the answer is 'Saying'.

When it is so and happiness is the ultimate objective of all that we do, my question is "how many times do we utter the word 'happy' in a day?" Two, three, four or maximum five times such as Happy Birthday, Happy Anniversary. In a year we say Happy New Year, Happy Holi, Happy Diwali, Happy Pongal etc. It adds up to only a few times that we utter the word 'happy' despite having 365 days.

What if we say this word 'HAPPY' many more times in a day? When many participants ask me what will happen if we do it, my response is, 'try & experience for yourself.' As for me, I have been doing it for more than two decades!

My next question is how we start the day. The answer I receive is, "by saying good morning." My suggestion is to start by wishing "happy morning" at the start of the day. Even better is to wake up happily which will make it easier to wish by saying "**Happy Morning!**"

Obviously, the question that arises is, 'Why should we wake up happily?'

I suggest that we must wake up not just happily but with gratitude because we are also lucky to see the new day. There are many not so fortunate, who pass away in the night and are not able to see this morning.

Also, if one starts a day happily, the possibility of the whole day being happier is greater. Why? By waking up happily, we increase the chances of the day being happier. When the day is happier, there are more chances of the evening being happier which will make the night more peaceful and in turn the next morning happier. If we continue it day in and day out, the impact can be on our entire life will be happy. It has been for me.

Waking up happily is also definitely easier than being happy in another moment of the day. This is because at that time we are only with ourselves and later people/situations we come in contact with, can impact our happiness.

Also, when I ask participants how many of them have to get up in the morning which means actually, they do not wish to, but they do get up to carry out tasks for the day. There are many who raise their hands in affirmation. To this my response is two things: one, anything done with compulsion will never be done happily and second, we must refrain from saying we should start waking up happily as 'should' is prescriptive and normally used when we want others to do something. Therefore, we must refrain from using words like 'have to' and 'should' and substitute these with:

I can do it, I will do it, I will continue doing it .....

e.g. you can chant:

I can wake up in the morning happily.

I will wake up happily in the morning.

I will continue waking up happily in the morning. (of course, only till the day God takes us away)

"CAN" is Belief....

"WILL" is Commitment ....

"WILL CONTINUE" helps one to sustain. (Sustaining a new practice will finally make it a habit– one that we do effortlessly.)

The taste of food is in eating. Reflect, how will we feel, if we start our day happily with positive energy and remain charged with it till people or situations affect it.

Sleeping well uninterruptedly in the night, will be helpful and for which not being with any electronic gadget at least one hour before bedtime, going to bed with good positive thoughts, meditating for few minutes before sleeping and living the present day creating happy memories and recalling these before sleeping etc. can help.

An interesting intervention helped me start my morning happily and is also helping many others. It is simple, I send Happy Morning messages along with one positive thought in Hindi and one in English to dozens of my friends and relatives and in turn they also respond with positive messages and happy wishes for me. In addition, I have a WhatsApp group of participants who have attended my workshops and share with them positive messages. Over the years they remain connected with me this way and by wishing Happy Morning they are also reminding themselves to start their morning happily.

What we read, write, speak, listen to, and see affects our subconscious mind. Thus, happily wishing any time of the day creates positive energy. Many people say that helping others through acts of charity or volunteer work makes them feel better and happier. New research goes further and finds that simply wishing someone well has a similarly positive effect on our moods. Another way to boost self-esteem and improving mental wellness is to start the morning with positive affirmations. Positive affirmations are made up of phrases that you can say aloud to yourself or in your head. Some of these affirmations are:

I am grateful for being alive on a new day.
I believe in myself.
I am the best.
I can do it.
Therefore Success Mantra-1 is
"Waking up happily in the morning."

2

BEING
LIVELY

Success Mantra - 2
Being Lively

Success is what is sought by all, but each has his own a definition for it. For someone getting a degree is success, for another person getting a job is success, for yet another getting a car, a house or amassing wealth is success. Also at different ages, success gets a new meaning, such as at age three, speaking and walking could be considered success, at age thirteen, passing high school, at age eighteen, getting a degree, at age twenty-two getting a job and at age sixty keeping oneself in good health.

But when it comes to Life as such, what really is success? I found an interesting definition that **"Success is Successful Living."** And what is successful living? **Successful living is when for most of our stay on this earth, we are happy, healthy and lively.**

Being happy is the sole objective of life in all circumstances, good or bad, favourable or unfavourable. Happiness has nothing to do with success, achievement or what one has in life or what one possesses. I have met umpteen people, who have all these. but are still miserable. This amplifies the importance of Successful Living rather than having a Successful Life. We will delve on happiness in life in greater detail when we discuss Living Life.

Being healthy is most necessary as health is the prime factor for living a beautiful life. Everything becomes meaningless, money, promotions etc when health is gone. Also, happy people are healthy people and healthy people are happy people.

Being Lively is a must for living. Being lively is being full of life all the time, which means being full of energy, enthusiasm & passion.

Interestingly, renowned personalities in the past and present might

21

be successful in their own domain but more importantly they are happy, healthy and lively people. To name a few, APJ Abdul Kalam in the field of space technology, Amitabh Bachchan in acting, Sachin Tendulkar in cricket, Sania Mirza in lawn tennis and P.V. Sindhu in badminton have excelled in their own field.

The attributes are the same for every one of them & other successful people. They have all faced challenges of life, most adverse conditions but happily came out of these. They enjoyed good health throughout their life. Those who are alive even now are still enjoying good health. They are energetic, enthusiastic and above all passionate about what they do.

Energy is the capacity to do work, Enthusiasm is looking forward to any situation with excitement and Passion is a strong internal desire to achieve any objective.

Energy and enthusiasm deplete with time, but passion keeps adding fuel to these, thereby keeping energy and enthusiasm intact irrespective of time. Passion is the power that comes from focusing on what excites one.

Being Lively contributes to everything we do, day in and day out. This is a sign of living. Lively people are bubbling with life and wherever they go infuse others also to be charged. These are people whose company is sought by all and at all places. It is not that such people do not have challenges in life. They can meet these challenges more effectively because of the energy, enthusiasm and passion they have. Lively people are excited about life and make the most of every moment. They usually excel in whatever they do. A lively person has an energetic personality, is always alert and prefers being active as opposed to just hanging around. Such people are keenly alive and spirited. In one word they can be described as fully engaged with life instead of simply existing.

A lively person is typically full of life, positive, high-spirited and animated. They often have a cheerful and enthusiastic demeanour, and they tend to bring energy and excitement to social interactions. They are generally engaging and enjoy being the center of attention in social settings.

Anyone of us can be lively by practicing the following attributes:

1. Cultivate positivity: focus on positive thinking and develop an optimistic outlook. Make a conscious effort to see the bright side of situations and maintain a positive attitude.

2. Take care of yourself: prioritize self-care to boost your energy levels and overall well-being. Get enough sleep, eat a balanced diet, exercise regularly and engage in activities that bring you joy.

3. Embrace enthusiasm: approach activities with enthusiasm and passion. Find things that genuinely excite you and pursue them wholeheartedly. Let your enthusiasm shine through in your words, actions and interactions with others.

4. Be present: be fully present in each moment. Engage actively in conversations and show genuine interest in others. Being fully present allows you to connect more deeply with people and experiences.

5. Step out of your comfort zone: challenge yourself to try new things and explore different experiences. Pushing beyond your comfort zone can help you discover new passions.

6. Surround yourself with positive influences: surround

yourself with people who exude positivity and energy. Their enthusiasm can be contagious and inspire you to become more vivacious.

7. Express yourself: find creative outlets to express yourself through art, music, dance, writing or any other medium. Allow free expression of your emotions and passions.

8. Maintain a sense of humour: develop a light-hearted and playful approach to life. Embrace humour and find joy in laughter. Don't take yourself too seriously and learn to find amusement in everyday situations.

Here is an interesting example from my Workshop for Hostel Wardens of the Tribal Welfare Department of the Government of MP. In each hostel, there are fifty students studying in various classes. These students are from economically disadvantaged backgrounds and are generally very subdued in nature. After the concept of being lively was shared with the hostel wardens they were charged and shared the same with the students. Consequently, the activities of the hostel got a boost and now children start their morning with exercise and a group dance too, which shows their energy, enthusiasm and passion and remain charged all through the day. These are available on my YouTube channel titled **Seekho aur Seekhao, Mulywaan Ban Jao...** Do see for yourself and feel the highly charged environment.

Therefore Success Mantra 2 is
Being Lively

3

Value Addition to be

VALUABLE

+
X
??
1   1=11

Success Mantra - 3
Value Addition to be **VALUABLE**

The journey of life has three components: **Knowing yourself, Deciding where you wish to take your life** and **Living the journey.** Let us understand each in detail.

1. **Knowing yourself** means knowing where you are. This is the starting point hence quite critical. What does knowing self mean?

It means knowing your strengths, your areas of improvement (weakness is a negative word that is de-motivating, while area of improvement implies you cannot do it now yet indicates the possibility of getting it done by improving) Finally, your potential is the maximum capacity of your contribution in any area. To know your potential, you must stretch, and stretch without stress. Stretching is challenging and you must break all shackles. Everyone around you and the world too puts these shackles by saying, "you cannot do it or you are not worthy of it." But these are not as dangerous as those which you put on yourself by saying, "I cannot do it, I am not worthy." Without breaking these shackles, you really cannot move forward in life. This is essential to move towards growth. Only by trying what you have not done before, you will know your capabilities.

To quote Darwin P Kingsley: **"You have powers you never dreamed of. You can do things you never thought you could do. There are no limitations in what you can do, except the limitation of your own mind."**

2. **Deciding where you want to take your life :** means deciding the aim of life and taking it there. This is necessary, otherwise life will take you where it wishes to take you and you will keep wondering where you have come.

Goals are very helpful to decide the destination. Imagine a game of football where the goal posts shift every now and then.

Goals are the road maps that guide you and show you what is possible for your life – Les Brown

Brian Tracy says, **"Goals in writing are dreams with deadlines."**

I love what Davis Waitley says, which helped me in my own life, **"Goals provide the energy source that powers our lives."**

Looking back, all my life I had dreamt of developing a Training and Development Institute and a learning culture as Training Manager in NTPC. I organized events that were never done or not done to scale in NTPC projects and stations where I served. A unique culture was established at the Textile Plant. I steered shop floor initiatives at the Indore Management Association – this intervention was initiated for the first time in India and was continued for many years nurturing organizational development in various partnering enterprises and institutions.

But what gave me immense happiness and fulfillment was seeing the visible outcomes while facilitating the building of a happiness culture in H&R Johnson, NMDC and Tribal Welfare Department, Madhya Pradesh and many other organizations. With these partners, my association was for three years or more.

I felt elated when people coached and assisted by me attained their own potential, achieved success for themselves and helped organizations they were working with to optimize effectiveness. I dreamt of an outcome almost invariably, made specific goals to be achieved, planned the steps and felt happy that measurable, definite success was achieved. Therefore, the determination of where one wishes to take one's life is crucial.

3.   **Living the journey:** the third and final step in the journey of life is to live the journey and not do it mechanically. I am pained to

observe those who live their life as Calendars. Each day is ticked off by ticking the date, the page is torn after the month passes and the calendar is changed after completion of the year. Thus, they lead a routine and boring life.

Living life is living every moment happily and doing something in the present moment that can result in greater happiness in moments to come. A most appropriate quote, **"All of us die but not all of us live."** It is your life, and you must take responsibility for it. You can, if you wish, make living itself a journey of development.

Next, let us have a look at the processes of development. A bud grows into a flower through its own process of development and a caterpillar transforms into a butterfly through its own process. The difference between the journey of the development of a bud to a flower and a caterpillar to a butterfly are vital. While a bud grows into a flower through a natural process of development, a caterpillar develops into a butterfly through stages which are painful. Not all caterpillars grow to become butterflies, as many perish in the struggle itself.

Most notable is Late A.P.J. Kalam, who became the topmost space scientist though born in a very simple family. All over the world there have been many who transformed their lives and became top leaders in industry, business, politics, sports, theatre etc. Around us too, we can see many who went through the transformation process and today are creating a name for themselves.

Change can be reversed but transformation is irreversible. The journey of transformation is more important than the destination. Since you are going through this book, I can say for you that you can, you will & you can continue to transform. Have faith in yourself, decide goals for your life and transform to get your dreams fulfilled.

Let us now understand how the process of transformation takes place. It is again in three simple steps:

Learning, Growth / Development, Success.

Learning

Growth / Development

Success

Learning:

When we arrive in this world, we know nothing but gradually we learn and can do many things. Thus, learning leads to growth and development which finally leads to success; the ultimate purpose of everything we undertake. The root of all success lies in learning and learning alone.

Learning can be only in three areas; **Knowledge , Skill and Attitude.** (I learnt this almost five decades back in a workshop at NITIE, Mumbai) and have not been able to find any other area. All learning can be in only one of these, Knowledge or Skill or Attitude; or in combinations of two, such as knowledge and skill, skill and attitude or knowledge and attitude or in all three of these knowledge, skill, and attitude but no fourth area is there for learning.

Let us now understand each area of learning:

Knowledge is a gathering of facts and information. Knowledge can be obtained through books or internet.

Skill is developing expertise in any act or trade and comes by practice.

Attitude is the way one looks at things and the meaning one gives to these. It is exhibited in one's way of thinking, feeling or behavior.

While knowledge is useful to you only in limited aspects, acquiring skills is more important than acquiring knowledge. However, your attitude decides the altitude you will go up to and is most critical in life. Anais Nin says, **"We don't see the world as it is, we see the world as we are."** So true, thus attitude plays a vital part in your journey of life and in your journey of transformation. Attitude is formed by your perceptions which are often formed by your experience. When your experiences are limited, many times your perceptions are biased thereby limiting your attitude.

You start seeing limited possibilities, limited solutions to challenges posed by life and with a narrow attitude, your life itself becomes limited. This throttles growth, curtails desire to learn and prevents new experiences and new perceptions. Life just keeps moving within a limited area and tends to stagnate. Depression and disenchantment with life are natural consequences. What a waste of this valuable life?

A beautiful story explains this well: **There was a fisherman, he had a small boat and was using it to catch fish in the river and earn a livelihood for himself and his family. To augment his income in his spare time he started ferrying villagers across the river to the opposite bank. One day a few tourists came there and asked him to give them a boat ride for an hour, for which they paid him well. Now he was catching fish, ferrying villagers, and offering boat rides to tourists, thus increasing his income.**

One day he had a large catch of fish, ferried a lot of villagers and tourists, and made a substantial earning. In the evening, he brought his boat to the shore and tied it with a rope to a pole and went home happily with the day's income. Reaching home, he asked his wife and children to pack some food and

musical instruments, so that they could enjoy an all-night boat ride, eat and have fun.

Everyone was happy and they came to the boat, began playing their instruments, singing, dancing, eating, and having fun. The fisherman took the oars and kept rowing the boat. After midnight, they were all tired, including the fisherman and went to sleep on the boat itself.

On waking up in the morning, the fisherman found he had forgotten to untie the boat the previous night, so in the darkness he kept rowing his boat in an area limited by the length of rope with which the boat was tied to the pole."

Like the fisherman, when you have a narrow attitude, you forget to untie the rope and with limited experiences, perceptions, and attitude, you see limited possibilities and life loses its meaning and purpose.

You must untie the rope from the pole and take your boat of life to new shores, to have new experiences and even take it into the sea to attain greater heights by expanding your mindset to transform your life.

Again, attitude can be positive or negative. A negative attitude will make you see everything as a problem and find fault everywhere. On the other hand, a positive attitude will help you see an opportunity in every challenge; come up with multiple solutions for a single problem and help you make the best choice. Thus, a broad and positive attitude does wonders and paves the path to success.

If you are asked whether whatever you have learnt in life is somewhat good, you will respond with an affirmation. Similarly, if you were asked if whatever you have done in life till now is somewhat good, you will affirm that too. However, if you were asked if whatever you have learned in life till now or done in life till now, is sufficient, your answer will be a 'no'. This leads to the conclusion that you have to learn more and do more.

The process of learning more and doing more and better is called Value Addition.

Value addition makes you more valuable, which leads to greater success. You play many roles in life and in each role, you do not decide how valuable you are. That decision is made by the ones with whom you play the role. Thus, how valuable a son is as perceived by his parents, a father by his children, a manager by his associates and a teacher by his students. Therefore, although we all wish to be considered valuable, it is not in our hands. However, value addition, learning more and doing more and better is entirely in our hands.

Learning is a continuous process that happens throughout our lives – having a curious mind is going to lead us to new and changing horizons. But applying the learning in practice i.e. Value Addition ensures reaching our full potential in all aspects.

It is beautifully illustrated by the story "**The Marble Tile and The Statue.**"

In a hall, there was a marble statue and on the floor were marble tiles. People came from long distances and folded their hands, paying homage to the statue.

One night when the hall was closed, a tile said to the statue, "This is injustice." When asked by the statue what the injustice was, the tile responded, "People fold their hands before you, but they stand on top of me." The statue said "Sister! we are from same ore." To which the tile exclaimed, "That's why it is a greater injustice."

On hearing this, the statute responded, "Remember the day, the sculptor came with his chisel and hammer. When he came to you, you hardened yourself. He came to me frustrated and I

33

suffered all his strokes and became a statue, but you did not and were sent to the tile factory and became a tile."

It is true that the learning is hard and painful but all your sculptors, parents, teachers, trainers (and even life) keeps trying to help you learn by sharing their learning, received by them the hard way and it is up to you how much you learn from everyone and from each experience. **The things that hurt also instruct - greater the pain, greater the lesson.** Failures are an essential part of learning and success too, therefore, **"Learn to fail or fail to learn."**

Quoting Elbert Hubbard, **"The greatest mistake a man can make is to be afraid of making one."** Failures are the steppingstones to success and are better teachers than success. Continuous value addition also boosts our self-confidence, helps us to keep pursuing our personal and professional development goals, leading to all achievements, which are a great source of happiness.

Scientific studies have shown that lifelong learning activates the functioning of the brain and slows the aging process. Utilizing this learning for remaining healthy, spirited, and useful for others also keeps boredom at bay.

Therefore, Value Addition is **"a process that leads to change, which occurs as a result of experience and increases the potential for improved performance and future learning."** (Ambrose et al, 2010, p. 3).

Only by going through this process of value addition, will you be considered Valuable. Unfortunately, everyone desires to be valuable but only few achieve it by value addition - once you have this, victory is at your feet.

Therefore Success Mantra-3 is
Value Addition to be Valuable

Success Mantra

4

Living
LIFE

Living Life

Success Mantra - 4
Living Life

"It is not the years in your life but the life in your years that counts."

-Adlai Stevenson

A question which I invariably ask in my Workshops is, **"if Earning a living, Passing life & Living life, are all the same?** Suddenly everyone realizes and responds that these are not the same.

Earning a living is making money to meet daily needs such as food, shelter etc. and is necessary but cannot be termed as living. It starts with earning a living and then it becomes accumulating money. There are many who are so busy only with making money that they forget even living life.

Passing life is wasting time and simply going from one day to another without doing anything worthwhile.

If you love life, don't waste time, for time is what life is made up of – Bruce Lee

Living life, as we all now know, is living every moment and doing something in that moment, that makes the next moment happier. While living life, we get engaged with it fully and invest time and efforts for a useful pursuit. Since essentially life is time, when we are living life, we are filled with positive emotions in each moment and engaged in actions that give meaning to life.

Live life to the fullest because it only happens once - Maddi Jenkins

Happiness is a pursuit which everyone engages in but happiness is not found, it has to be created for self and others. Rightly said, **"Happiness is not a destination, it is the journey of life."**

Often happiness is confused with pleasure, while both are distinctly different. Pleasure is focused on things; happiness focuses on people. Pleasure is short term while if we live one happy moment, its memory can make us happy for a lifetime. Pleasure is external and happiness is internal. Pleasure may require money, but happiness is free. The next important distinction is pleasure can result in pain, but happiness only multiplies resulting in greater happiness.

"How we spend our days is, of course, how we spend our lives," said Annie Dillard

If all this is so simple, why do people become unhappy. There are many reasons, but the most common are three:

1. We do not live in the moment, we either brood over the past or worry about the future. We do not remember days, we remember moments.

   Oprah Winfrey said, **"Living in the moment means letting go of the past and not waiting for the future. It means living your life consciously, being aware that each moment you breathe is a gift."**

2. What we have is not of much value to us but what others have is more valuable to us. The paradox is that most of the time we value things or people, only after they are not with us. The tendency to value things when we don't have them or when we lose them is often related to the psychological phenomenon known as 'scarcity.' When something is scarce or unavailable to us, we tend to perceive it as more valuable and desirable.

3. We keep comparing ourselves with those who have more than us in any respect. We forget that the life we are living now is what millions are dreaming of.

The process of happiness is simple as given below:

- **We all want to be happy.**

- **For being happy we must make others happy**

- **For making others happy we must be happy**

The essence is happy people make others happy and vice versa.

Happiness is Positive Energy

This came to mind while responding to a participant in a short session on happiness. A few years back I was at Bhilai, where I was interacting on happiness with the senior plant personnel of SAIL. After the session, one of the participants said, "I liked the session and learned some nice concepts about happiness but please tell me, if my health is bad, my relationships are not good, my work is boring, my boss does not like me, then, how can I be happy?

I had been conducting these sessions for more than two decades, but this was the first time such a question was posed to me.

I responded almost instantly, "supposing you fall in a very deep pit………. and then I realized that if I am giving an example which is of an unpleasant situation, I should use myself as the example. So, I rephrased my response and said, "supposing I fall into a very deep pit, will I require more or less energy to come out?" Immediately, he smiled and responded, "obviously more."

Then I said, "Happiness is not smiling & laughing. Happiness is positive energy and when challenges of life are putting us down from all sides, we need more of it."

This realization became my learning for life too and is helping me even now to meet challenges of life.

Train your mind to see the good in everything. Positivity is a choice. The happiness of your life depends on the quality of your thoughts.

Live life to the fullest and focus on the positive. What we think decides our happiness. Positive thinking does not mean absence of problems or denial of the same, but it means acceptance of problems and finding solutions with positive thinking. Positive thinking helps one to remain focused and charged thereby doing one's best to meet the challenge. Positive Thinking is thus immensely important.

Positive thinking leads to positive actions, positive actions lead to positive habits and positive habits lead to positive outcomes.

For Positive Thinking:

- **Believe in Self:** Have faith in your abilities. This is the starting point for moving ahead on your journey of success.

- **Stop complaining**: Complaining only harms one who complains. Be a part of the solution, not a part of the problem.

- **Don't worry, be happy**: Worry is a waste of energy and weakens self.

- **Expect the best and get it**: You've got to win in your mind before you win in your life, and it certainly pays.

- **Never accept defeat**: Falling is an accident, staying down is a choice. Falling is part of life and getting back up is living.

The 12 Qualities of Happiness as brought out by Dan Baker

LOVE	OPTIMISM	COURAGE
A SENSE OF FREEDOM	PROACTIVITY	SECURITY
HEALTH	SPIRITUALITY	ALTRUISM
PERSPECTIVE	HUMOR	PURPOSE

The following can help you live life to the fullest:

- Listen to your inner being.

- Understand the power of authenticity, i.e. walk the talk

- Visualize your future self.

- Define your core values.

- Let beliefs lead to passion.

- Step out of your comfort zone and reach out eagerly and fearlessly for newer and richer experience.

- Help others.

All my life I did dream. Dreamt of my mission, my projects, my relationships and even my life. In my sessions also I ask my participants to dream and dream big. I strongly believe that dreams give meaning to life. Life without dreams is not worth living. Rightly said:

"Every morning you have two choices: continue to sleep with your dreams, or wake up and chase them."

What is important to understand that dreams do not work till we do. Hence, you cannot stop at dreaming only but must pursue dream realization too. These simple steps for this are:

- **DREAM:** Dream big as these are about you and your life.

- **BELIEVE:** Many dreams are strangulated by you immediately after seeing them when you tell yourself, 'you cannot do it' or 'these are too big to become a reality'.

- **DARE:** After all you dream of something which you have not done or not achieved. Therefore, it is an act of courage to dream of these things.

- **DO:** Action gives meaning to translate the dreams into reality. Only if you plant a seed, water it, give manure and nurture it, this will be a plant and tomorrow might give you fruits.

We have only one life and we decide how to live it. We can simply pass through it or live it to fullest by first dreaming of it and then making these dreams a reality. Andy Andrews has rightly said - **"Life itself is a privilege, but to live life to the fullest - well, that is a choice."**

Sadly, many do not exercise this choice and instead of living life fully they simply pass through it. To quote Oscar Wilde — **To live is the rarest thing in the world. Most people exist, that is all.**

He means most people do not have an enjoyable, high quality of life and do not fully live their lives. I am certain that you will make a choice to live life to the fullest by being engaged with it, taking its ownership, and trying new things every day, having new experiences by being happy and making everyone coming in your contact happy too.

Therefore, Success Mantra 4 is
Living Life by Being Happy and Making others Happy

5

Utilising the Law of
ATTRACTION

Utilising the Law of Attraction

Success Mantra - 5
Utilising the Law of **Attraction**

The Universe is made up of electromagnetic fields and all things have the power to attract. Everything that comes into your life, you have attracted magnetically. And given that your thoughts are also energy, with their own magnetic properties, it means that your thoughts attract things, your thoughts become things, and therefore your mind is responsible for the world around you. Your thoughts are drawing things into your life, just like a magnet. This universal law is known as the "LAW OF ATTRACTION."

"A lot of people are afraid to say what they want. That's why they don't get what they want.' Madonna – the iconic Super Star.

The truth is that people think more about what they do not want in their life unknowingly strengthening those thoughts. The Universe unfortunately does not bother as to what is good or bad for you, it simply responds to what you are thinking of. Suppose you come out of your house, and you have to reach some place on time, but you are all the time thinking that you might get late, then all the conditions you will meet on the road will only delay your reaching the destination.

Interestingly, a positive thought is a hundred times more powerful than a negative thought. However, there is a time delay between the thought and it getting converted into a thing, thereby giving you time to work on your thoughts or change or modify these. But at least 60000 thoughts come to your mind in one day. And with that many thoughts bouncing around in your head, it may seem very hard to control all of them. Fortunately, there is a simple thing that can be helpful to you. These are your feelings and what you can do, is to focus on how you're feeling.

When you're feeling good, you can't help but have these good thoughts. And those good thoughts attract more good thoughts and better feelings. And that sets up the attraction for all the good stuff to come your way. That's when you're on a roll, a lucky, perfect day.

Understand the importance of saying "Happy Morning." Starting your morning happily, you increase the possibilities of having a happy day. But if you are feeling stressed or depressed, that tells you that your thoughts are heading to the dark side. That often leads to a spiral of bad thoughts and bad feelings. Things go from bad to worse, and it is a vicious cycle that makes the day bad. Once you start the day with a negative thought, more bad thoughts and bad feelings get attracted, which then attract bad reactions, and suddenly your whole vibe becomes negative and you attract a chain of negative events.

So, if you ever find yourself having one of these days, you have to realize that it isn't caused by the bad stuff happening around you. That's just the effect. It's caused by your feelings and your own thoughts. And once you know that, you'll be able to turn a bad day around just by changing the way you're thinking and feeling. DOUBT, FEAR and INSECURITY are very strong negative feelings, which can ruin your day and even your life. On the contrary GRATITUDE, APPRECIATION & LOVE are very strong positive feelings that have the power to make your day beautiful and rewarding.

The idea is to stay aware, and to ask yourself, "How am I feeling now? What is my vibe like?" If you're buzzing with excitement, with abundance of energy, enthusiasm, passion, happiness, gratitude, you'll be attracting AWESOME stuff. But if you're feeling angry, unhappy, resentful, depressed, doubtful or fearful, your thoughts are totally bleak as a result you'll be attracting AWFUL stuff in your life at that moment.

Changing thoughts is challenging but the easier method is to be in touch with feelings and working on these to attract good in life.

Feelings create the mood. You're in a good mood when you have positive feelings and in a bad mood when you have bad feelings. You are generally always in touch with your mood and thus your feelings, more than your thoughts. What you can do is to change the mood. Simple ways that work are listening to good music, playing a sport, dancing, being with a toddler or else simply breathing in fresh air, feeling the sunshine, the wind in your hair or the rain on your skin.

I have consciously filled myself with gratitude by saying and writing, 'thank you, thank you, thank you,' and appreciating all things good in people and the environment. I constantly look for opportunities to say, "I love you" to express my love to people around and even to my own life. I have attracted good people, good circumstances, and good outcomes in my own life for decades by this simple application of the law by being in a good mood most of the time.

Another simple way to apply the law is to write down a list of things that bring a smile to your face every time you think of them. Anytime your mood is down, you're feeling stressed or depressed or angry or unhappy, look at your list and FEEL GOOD. I read an article about a lady, who took selfies every time she felt good and put it in a folder on her computer. Whenever she wanted to uplift her mood, she would glance at her own pictures in the folder and it helped.

ASK, BELIEVE & RECEIVE is the process to practice the law of attraction. Anything you earnestly wish for, you can ask the Universe, believe it is yours, envision that you have already received it and then actually receive it gratefully.

As to how much time it will take to fulfill your wish, by applying the law of attraction is between you and the Universe, however, a strong desire and complete faith will help.

The law works and my faith got strengthened because I came

across this article by Ms Aakansha Sharma in the ETimes of March 6th, 2024. I wished to list the points that will help in effective application of Secret and her article beautifully brings out these points as listed below:

1. **Positive Thinking**: By maintaining a positive mindset and focusing on that which you want, rather than what you don't want, you can attract positive outcomes into your life.

2. **Visualization:** Imagining that desired outcome has been already achieved, you can align your thoughts and actions with what you want to manifest.

3. **Gratitude**: By expressing gratitude for what you already have, you attract more abundance into your life.

4. **Having clarity**: Setting clear indications is important for manifesting your desires. Clearly define what you want to attract into your life, and then take actions towards these goals.

5. **Belief in self**: Believing in yourself and your ability to manifest your desires is very important. Confidence and self-belief help a lot.

6. **Don't limit yourself**: Limiting beliefs can block your ability to manifest your desires. Letting go of beliefs that no longer serve you and replacing them with ones that empower you, is the key to unlocking your full potential.

7. **Take action at the right time**: While positive thinking and visualization are important, taking inspired action towards your goals is critical, which will bring your desires into reality.

8. **Be mindful, be aware**: Constantly being in touch with your feelings by staying in the present and mindful, you

can consciously choose your thoughts and emotions that align with your desires.

9. **Be Patient**: Manifesting does not happen overnight. Desires are not fulfilled overnight. Patience and perseverance and trusting the process will make it happen.

10. **Sharing what you have**: Secret works only when you give back what you receive from the universe. By sharing your abundance and giving it back to others, you share your blessings that multiply and find their way back to you.

During the last two decades I have shared the law of attraction principle with thousands of my participants. Many of them, who correctly applied it, have transformed their life. I have personally benefitted by a simple application and utilization of the "Law of Attraction", which luckily, I was practicing unconsciously, even when I did not know about the law. (Incidentally, I chanced upon the book 'Secret' by Rhonda Byrne only two decades ago and I would love to say I attracted this long back into my life.) The ten points brought out in Ms Sharma's article have been practiced by me for decades and my wishes were converted into reality by manifesting the law. Some of these I will now talk about.

The law of attraction has filled my life with amazing achievements. Whether it was establishing an Institute of Training & Development at NTPC Shakti Nagar, building robust processes of training that stood the test of time, turned around a power plant from UPSEB at Unchahar(UP), developing sensitivity to needs of patients and their attendants at the M.Y. Medical College, Indore, contributing to building a totally new work culture at a textile plant at Indore, Mentoring & Coaching at H& R Johnson Tile Plant at PEN, Raigad, initiating the happy culture at RAMCO, Chennai, developing a happy, positive and performing organizational culture at NMDC, Hyderabad and initiating interventions of happy and positive culture at JPL Tamnar,

Chhattisgarh besides interventions at numerous institutions and organizations, everywhere the law of attraction worked for me in enlisting support of stakeholders and top leadership too. Many of these interventions created history by being the first of its kind in the country. The most recent example is of Tribal Welfare Department, where I was associated for three years, and the participating hostel wardens created a Seekho Sikhao culture in their hostels. Innovative practices were adopted by them and this intervention, to my knowledge, is first of its kind in any Government Department and in any State of this country. All these success stories reinforced my belief in the law and encouraged me to apply the law in all endeavors, small or big. The images conceived by me became a reality due to the reinforcing force from the Universe. The law has given me wonderful friends, I have received love and affection from many and support for my initiatives. I feel truly blessed and grateful. The publishing of this book in association with my Editor is the latest good thing, I attracted in my life by application of this law.

Anyone can apply the law of attraction to make life better by feeling good, remaining filled with positive feelings, being in a good mood and pursuing those activities that make one feel better.

Therefore, Success Mantra 5 is
Utilizing The Law of Attraction

(Videos explaining the law of attraction can be accessed on YouTube. "Law of Attraction: first 20 minutes" brings out the gist of the principle).

HOUSE VS HOME OF LIFE

Twenty-five years back my son who was studying at IIM Calcutta shared a story with me by which I was awe struck. A simple one-page story which impacted me and made me look at life with a new perspective. Even my book, **"Jeevan Ke Rang, Khushiyon Ke Sang"** was written based on this story.

The Story goes like this. The context of the story is based in a foreign land, where wooden houses are made primarily because of frequent earthquakes.

In such a country, there was a Carpenter, who was working with a Contractor for more than two decades and thus developed great skills and constructed beautiful houses.

One day this Carpenter went to the Contractor and said, "I want to retire." Since he was such an experienced skilled worker, the Contractor asked if he wanted to retire because the remuneration was low. The Carpenter responded with a "No."

Then the Contractor asked, "How will you make a living?" The Carpenter replied that he had acquired a small piece of land on which he would grow vegetables and earn his living by selling these.

The Contractor asked, "What will you do? "The Carpenter replied, "I will play with my grandchildren and spend quality time with my family."

Once the Contractor realized that the Carpenter would not continue working, he asked him to make one last house for him, to which the Carpenter reluctantly agreed only because of their long association.

The Carpenter went to store and brought whatever wood was available, without bothering about the quality of wood and started making the house. Normally, he was very particular about the quality of wood but not this time.

The Carpenter did not put his heart into the work and somehow completed the house and sent a message to the Contractor to take over the house and relieve him.

The Contractor entered the house and declared, "Friend! because of you, I have made a lot of money, so this house is my gift to you."

Now the Carpenter was shocked and said to himself "What a big mistake, I have made? I made beautiful houses for others.

Had I known I was constructing this house for myself, I would have used better quality wood and utilized all my skills to do a great job." However, now the Carpenter had to live in the house gifted to him.

This story ended with a powerful message - like the Carpenter, many of us often pass through life as if it is not our own. We waste time and are not happy, we do not live fully, do not value-add, do not learn to build good relationships or find a purpose for our life. Life comes to an end one day, no matter how we have lived it. Life is ours and we must invest every moment of it in purposeful pursuit, learn and develop skills and attitudes to be valuable, build beautiful relationships, live every moment happily with energy, enthusiasm and passion and make our life meaningful for self and others. A very powerful lesson indeed!

This realization suddenly transformed my life and I decided to utilize every moment of my life and developed my mission of assisting others in attaining their potential in all areas of life. The journey that started 25 years back after this made me live a happier and more meaningful life and helped me touch thousands of lives. Participants of my Workshops ranged right from teenagers to senior citizen, from frontline associates to senior most leadership teams, students and teachers, ward boys, nurses to senior doctors, from organizations to institutions and from corporate to government departments. To my surprise, everyone related to this story and understood that this was the story not of the carpenter but of their life too.

After I share the story in my workshop, I ask participants if they will build a house of life or a home of life. Invariably, everybody's response is Home. When asked why, they admit that a house is only a structure built with bricks, cement, steel, mortar but a home is built with love and that's where we live. As a life without love, is not worth living. Reflecting on the story, I realized whether one is a billionaire or a pauper, whether it is house or home; life has only four areas of interface - **Self, Relationships, Work and Society**. This is the LIFE Cycle for each of us and our life moves from one area to another till we are alive.

By decorating each room, our life can become beautiful, by having love in each room, we can have a home of life; by planning for each room, we can plan our whole life. So simple - isn't it?

We will now visit each room and see how every room can be decorated and made beautiful to build a beautiful life.

6

Decorating the
ROOM OF SELF

Decorating the Room of Self

Success Mantra - 6
Decorating the **Room of Self**

Your Room of self is:
- **Your Behavior**
- **Your Nature**
- **Your Habits**
- **Your Thinking**
   &
- **Your Attitude**

In one word, it is termed as personality which identifies you and makes you unique, as no two people are exactly the same, not even twins.

Few interesting facts about the room of Self are:

For making it a part of your home of life, you must have love in this room. Therefore, loving self will be the starting point.

Room of Self is the most important part of your life as without decorating the room, you cannot decorate any other room. This is because you carry your behavior, nature, habits, thinking and attitude everywhere you go, whether in relationships, work or society. Every journey of life starts from here.

Interestingly, whatever you do in the day is only done because of your behavior, your nature, your habits, your thinking or your attitude. Every action is initiated, and every response is given only because of these.

We all get so busy improving the world around us that we often forget about improving self. Let us now understand each component that builds the room of self.

Behavior: is the way one acts or behaves. Good behavior generally refers to actions that are appropriate and respectful and that align with societal norms. Examples of good behavior include being respectful, following rules and laws, using good words, and taking responsibility for one's actions.

Bad behavior refers to actions that are harmful or disrespectful and that violate societal norms and values. Examples of bad behavior include being disrespectful, abusing, lying, bullying, breaking rules and laws, causing and hurting others by words or actions.

Behavior is something superficial and we exhibit our behavior differently with different people. We sometimes change our behavior even with the same individual if we expect something from him.

Nature: is much deeper and more intrinsic, it exhibits qualities or character of a person. A person with a good nature has a pleasant, cheerful disposition to please and be pleased, to accede to other's wishes and to overlook causes for offense.

Thus, synonyms of good nature are being gracious, pleasant, nice, amicable, sweet, friendly, cheerful, helpful, and kind. On the other hand, a person with a bad nature is unpleasant, disrespectable, unkind, rude, irritable, impolite, and inconsiderate.

Habits: are what we repeatedly do. We do it often and almost without thinking, so much so that these become an integral part of our self. A good habit takes time to be formed but we lose it easily. A bad habit is picked up easily, but it takes time to get rid of it.

Punctuality, self-discipline, exercising, eating healthy food, prioritizing, planning, being happy, learning something new, practicing gratitude are habits that can achieve success for us. Simple habits like drinking a good quantity of water, adequate sleep, saving etc. can make a big difference to one's life.

Bad habits are procrastination, being late, eating junk food, lying, not setting goals etc. and can result in disaster.

Thinking: could be positive or negative, broad, or narrow. Our thoughts build our world, thereby thinking positively we can have a beautiful world while the contrary is also true. With broad thinking we feel comfortable and can find solutions. With narrow thinking we are isolated and feel insecure and alone.

Attitude: is the way we look at anything and the meaning we give to it. Attitude is formed by our perceptions. Perception is the way we define anything for ourselves. Just as thinking, our Attitude can be positive or negative, healthy, or unhealthy. Healthy attitude is broad attitude and unhealthy attitude is narrow attitude.

With a healthy attitude, we have an open mind and are able to have new experiences, learn new things, meet new people thereby renewing our world constantly. With an unhealthy attitude, we have a closed mind making the possibilities less and our world limited. We live a mundane and routine life.

With a positive attitude problems become challenges thereby creating opportunities to learn, experience and grow. With a positive attitude, difficulties become steppingstones to success.

With a negative attitude, every problem is perceived bigger than what it really is. Our spirits become low, depression and anxiety weaken us, and we find ourselves helpless and unable to tap into the powers we have.

A healthy and positive attitude is the gateway to a new world, it opens new doors and keeps our spirits high. Our world keeps changing and life becomes meaningful.

Nature, Habits & Attitude are all critical attributes to decorate our room of self but only after building a healthy and positive attitude can we really develop.

Personality: the different qualities of a person that make one different from others is the summation of one's behavior, nature, habits, thinking & attitude. Therefore, every one of us has a unique and different personality.

Behavior is the outer component of one's personality while nature, habits, thinking, and attitude form the core. By superficial component i.e. behavior one can impress others, while it takes nature, habits, thinking & attitude to influence someone. Impressing people is short term while influencing people is more lasting and they are motivated to be like us.

If we work on our personality both outer & core, we can decorate the room of self and as we have seen this will impact all other rooms of our life such as relationship, work & society. To make it a room of the home of life and not a house of life, we need to love ourselves as only then we can love others.

Self-care does not mean being selfish. It means we constantly work to improve our behavior, nature, habits, thinking & attitude which paves the way to improving our relationships, our work, and any other interface.

Lao Tzu has beautifully said:

"Knowing others is intelligence,

Knowing yourself is wisdom,

Mastering others is strength,

Mastering yourself is true power."

Decorating room of self is Personal Development that takes to gain a deeper understanding of yourself including your strengths, your areas of improvement, your beliefs, and your potential. This awareness enables you to make necessary changes in your behaviour, nature, habits, thinking and attitudes. These changes positively affect all your actions during the day resulting in better feelings, better relationships, and better outcomes.

Life is not about finding yourself. Life is about creating yourself.

- **G. B Shaw**

We need to do all we can for improving our self as it is our responsibility and also because:

1. After all, we take ourselves with us wherever we go. Whether you are growing greater at your strengths, reducing your liabilities or expanding what you are capable of, personal development is a path.

2. You need relationships and only by self-development can you improve existing relationships and foster new relationships.

3. You wish to excel in the job you do and the journey necessitates self-development.

4. You wish to contribute to Society and be recognised for this. Self-development can help in this too.

5. It's **a path of personal greatness** and a way to **be YOUR best**.

Luckily, this learning came to me at a very early stage of life and has helped me all these years. Let us be clear, Self-development is a continuous process and is the journey of life, the way of life and has no destination. I am still a traveller.

The following did help me moving forward on this journey:

1. Learning visualization techniques

2. Having positive thoughts

3. Meditation

4. Competing only with myself

5. Being persistent

6. Setting small challenges

7. Celebrating smallest victories

For Self-development you have to Dream big, develop yourself, unleash your potential, play well with others, play to your strengths, enjoy the process share your unique gifts with the world, and grow your greatness by testing yourself, expanding yourself, learning and improving.

Whatever the mind of man can conceive and believe, it can achieve - Napoleon Hill

Self-development is a process in which a person grows or changes and becomes more advanced through one's own effort. You are lucky if you get someone in life to motivate you to do so, however, all the choices for change and working for them are dependent on you alone.

Remember you are your best investment.

Therefore, Success Mantra 6 is

Decorating the Room of Self

7

Decorating the Room of
RELATIONSHIPS

Success Mantra - 7
Decorating the Room of **Relationships**

Life starts with relationships and relationships are built by love. We love those whom we consider our own and the beauty is that we can consider anyone our own. This relationship though, starts with those with whom we have blood relations, but often does not get limited there. In fact, looking back we can easily observe the people with whom we build relationships in life (often beyond blood relationship) many a time become much closer. This is because while we receive blood relations by birth, friends we make by choice. A relationship is the bond between two people and often this bond is stronger with friends than even with those who are distantly connected with us through birth.

The sad part is, with joint families becoming rare, the family is getting limited to fewer members. Migration to new places in our own country and even outside is one major factor in weakening the bond between blood relatives.

For a strong relationship, love, trust, and communication are the most important constituents.

Love cements relationships. But love is not limited to feeling, Stefen Covey has beautifully said, "Love is a Verb." For love, we need to sacrifice, listen, appreciate, affirm and empathize.

Trust gets built when actions meet words, there is a saying, **"Trust takes years to build, seconds to break and forever to regain."** So true!

"A relationship without trust is like a cell phone without a network, all you can do is to play games."

However, communication is the glue for relationships. Honest, constant and transparent communications are the essence of a strong relationship. Invariably broken communication results in broken relationships.

Friendship is a beautiful relationship that is very dear to us because we choose it. **"I went out to find a friend, but I could not find one anywhere, but I went out to be a friend and I found many,"** is a beautiful quote that has inspired me to make so many friends.

Stephen Covey, I quote once again, has said when two people connect, they open an Emotional Bank Account (EBA) with each other. Just as for keeping a normal bank account operative we must maintain a balance in it, the same is true for EBA. If we only withdraw on from a bank account, the balance becomes zero and the account inactive. Therefore, we must keep depositing continuously to keep the account activated. This applies to EBA too.

There are six major deposits in EBA as prescribed by Stefen Covey:

Understanding the individual, attending to little things, keeping commitments, clarifying expectations, showing personal integrity by walking the talk and apologizing sincerely when you make a withdrawal.

In relationships, it can be observed that we are very careful with strangers so as not to make a withdrawal, however it is not so in close relationships. We often, maybe, unintentionally, keep making withdrawals.

Ella Wheeler Wilcox says beautifully, **"We flatter those we scarcely know; we please the fleeting guest. And deal full many a thoughtless blow, to those who love us best."**

Thus, to keep the EBA balance so that relationships are intact, we need to continuously keep making the above deposits. This will ensure that in a close relationship, even if a withdrawal is made when we do or say something that hurts, the EBA balance will be positive and the relationship will not be lost.

Though we are initiated into relationships in family, these are not limited to it. In the workplace, society and everywhere, relationships make a lot of difference to our happiness and wellbeing.

In 2006, after working for five years for myself conducting workshops and having close interaction with participants both adults and children, I did a scientific study to find out attributes that decide happiness levels in life. The study, which was conducted on actual data of pre-workshop expectations, feedback of participants and commitments made by them to actions after the workshop, the following conclusion was drawn:

Happiness in life is a function of –

Self-Management X Quality of Relationships in life

Self-Management is decorating the room of self-i.e. improving behavior, nature, habits, thinking & attitude. And the quality of relationships is the strong bond with people in our life whether in family, at work or in society. Interestingly, these two factors also act upon each other thereby if Self-Management is done, relationships improve and conversely if the relationships improve, we are motivated to improve Self-Management.

The longest study, for more than 80 years, ever conducted on human happiness is by Dr Waldinger, Professor of Psychiatry, Harvard Medical School and author of an important book, **"The Good Life"** (published in 2023).

The Project has followed participants from adolescence into old age, collecting data on their physical and mental health, jobs, relationships and more. Based on the findings from the 80 year long Harvard Study of Adult Development, the simple yet surprising truth is revealed; that stronger the relationships, the more likely we are to live in happiness, satisfaction and lead overall healthier lives.

This Harvard study of people over 85 years, found the No.1 thing that makes us happy in life and helps us live longer, is Social Fitness. All this makes the importance of healthy and strong relationships abundantly clear.

Another study has brought out that there are three types of fear:

Fear of natural calamities

Fear of wild animals

Fear of inhuman conduct of fellow human beings

Fear from natural calamities and of wild animals has been taken care of largely by human beings, but the strongest fear is that of inhuman conduct of fellow human beings that prevails even today.

An action is considered inhumane whenever someone acts without considering the discomfort or pain caused to another person or animal.

Another research has arrived at the conclusion that, **"Unhappiness at workplace/life is because of the Lack of Physical Facilities or Lack of Relationships."** Physical facilities have improved a lot at the workplace as well as in life, thus it can be said that unhappiness is mostly because of lack of relationships.

"People come on your side if they know you are in their side." Also, **"I do not care how much you know, if I do not know how much you care."**

Relationships give an opportunity to make a difference in the life of others and to one's own life. My own experience of last two decades of interactions with numerous participants working in Corporate (both public & private sectors) Government departments, schools, hospitals and informal sectors has significantly brought out, that where people understood the importance of relationships and worked for having better relationships at the work place, the productivity & quality in the organization improved and everyone had more positive feelings for each other and for their work too.

There is one mighty challenge in keeping relationships intact and that is Reaction.

When someone does not do what we would like him to do, and if the situation is not to our liking, we react. The thoughtless instantaneous action is Reaction. Reactions are major spoilers of relationships and situations.

The solution is simple. Instead of reacting, we need to Respond. A response is a carefully chosen alternative out of those available to us and which we get by asking ourselves, **"What can I do?"** It is the best course of action in a situation which is not to our liking or when the opposite person is doing what we do not like.

The process is that in such an event, we must press the Pause Button. No action is the best action in the moment when we are emotionally disturbed by a person not doing what we wish or the situation is not to our liking. When we get emotionally stable after a lapse of time, by asking ourselves what all we can do, we get many alternatives which can be termed as responses. We then choose the best response which is possible for us. Response is a carefully chosen delayed action and is the best we can do in such a situation.

Response + Able = Responsible, and the ability to choose a response is responsibility. Responsibility is not what others give to us; it is what we choose for ourselves.

By being responsive we inculcate an attitude of ownership, thereby we are neither a victim of actions of others nor a controller of others. I take responsibility for my life and accept outcomes of conscious choices and actions made by exercising my own free will. The essential factor for unhappiness is resistance and for happiness it is acceptance. Acceptance of self and others helps in building beautiful relationships, helping us to live a happy life.

When I reflect, I realise that I have been benefitted immensely by the relationships that were built by collaboration. I always believed that relationships should not be developed with a motive to gain. Let selfless relationships develop without any motives and benefits will follow naturally. This is validated by the fact that for last two decades, I am working for myself and never had to ask for work and have been reasonably engaged with challenging assignments. On the personal front my three doctors, whom I met professionally turned out to be my well-wishers and do everything to keep me healthy and fit. Dr Pradeep Mehta, leading physician at Indore, Dr Rama Krishna Gedela HOD (Physiotherapy and Wellness) at AIG Hospital, Dr Sandeep Nalla, Prosthodontics and Dr Bala Naga Sindhura, Dermatologist Star Hospitals not only respond to me anytime but also provide personalised care to anyone referred by me. They are all very busy professionals but make time for me. There are numerous incidents, where my relationships, helped me come out of a challenging situation happily or supported me at crucial times.

We can therefore conclude that relationships are crucial for a happy life and strong relationships go a long way in contributing to successful living.
Rightly said, **"No significant learning occurs without a significant relationship."**

Therefore, Success Mantra 7 is:
Decorating the Room of Relationships

8

Cleaning the

ROOM OF SOCIETY

Cleaning the Room of Society

We all expect Society to do a lot for us, but we fail to contribute to Society most of the times. How beautiful it would be if each one of us asked ourselves, "What are we doing for Society?"

Society for us, are the people who are connected to us in life beyond relationships.

We keep postponing any participation in Society on the pretext that we are engaged with family and work and thus do not have time for it. In my workshops when I ask, "Supposing in our house, we have a room, which we have kept locked for 30/35 years and then go and try to open the lock, will we be able to open it? The response is mostly no. Then I state that even if we break the lock of such a room which we have kept locked for years, what will we find? The response is always dirt, dampness, garbage, foul smell etc.

Now if we reflect on the house of life, we find Society full of bad elements, vices and wrongdoings. After all our Society is comprised of us and everyone with whom we come in contact on a day to day basis. Since we and everybody else are not doing anything to contribute to making it better, we obviously will have a Society that we will not be comfortable with. We do not get what we wish, we get what we deserve. While everyone complains of ill doings in Society around us, few do anything to change the situation and Society keeps deteriorating.

I am reminded of a beautiful story in this context. There was a king, who was very proud of his citizens. Once his friend, another king from the neighborhood was visiting him and he mentioned his pride to the visiting king. Then his friend asked him to test his people. A newly dug pond was there, and he advised the king to get an announcement made to his people that every household was to place a pot of milk in the pond in the night. In the morning when both the kings went to the pond, they found it filled with water only. On enquiry, it was found that everyone thought others would put milk so if one puts a pot of water, it will not be noticed. And the pond was full of water instead of milk.

When it comes to Society, everyone acts in a similar manner. People say it is the job of the Government to work for the welfare of Society. The Government feels it should be done by officers of the State. The State feels it should be done by village panchayats and local bodies, feel it should be done by the people. The circle gets completed and the welfare of Society remains unattended. Everyone complains Society is going from bad to worse but hardly anyone does anything as part of their responsibility.

The obvious question that will come to mind is, 'How can I as an individual affect Society ?' The answer is also simple.

As history shows us, an individual can dramatically shape Society and even the entire world. What follows are two examples of individuals who affected our world in a positive and a negative way. Adolfo Hitler is a sad example of an individual who brought about terrible consequences for many people and countries. In contradistinction, Martin Luther King Jr is a telling example of an individual whose contribution to the betterment of our world will never be forgotten.

During my workshops when the topic of Cleaning the Room of Society, I receive response like "We are working which takes a large amount of our time, then we have so many tasks to be done in household. For our children also a lot of attention and time is needed. Where do we have time, energy, and resources to work for society.' This is real and so I agree with them. However, then I ask them "What you are doing for living, if you do your best, will it increase profitability of the organization?" They affirm and then I ask, "Will it generate employment opportunities for regular and contract associates?'. They respond with yes. Then I share my contention with them that if each one does this in the organization, the organization will definitely do well, but it will also generate employment and that will be their contribution to society. Therefore, they do not have to make extra time for helping society and can do so simply by excellent contribution at work, for which, in any case, they are being paid too.

For having resources to help the society by a common man, I share my own experience. When I was 10 years old and my mother who was a religious person, was alive. One day a Sanyasi came and told her that he is getting a temple constructed and needed money for it. The Sanyasi gave my mother a 6 inch tin box with lid and arrangement for putting a small lock and asked her to keep putting in the box now and then any spare change. My mother kept doing so and the Sanyasi will come once every two months to collect the amount in box and take that against receipt too. After about two years, the Sanyasi stopped coming maybe because the temple was constructed but the box remained in household. My mother kept putting spare coins in the box and practice continued year to year. She will utilize the money to help some needy poor person. After her death, I left Allahabad, to join FCI and I took that box with me and kept it in my pooja. I also continued putting coins in the box and help some needy poor person. However, I changed the practice and started putting daily some amount in that and kept giving it to needy poor. Gradually my income increased and so the amount I was putting also increased and started putting both times when I went for prayers. Am humbled to say thousands of rupees kept getting accumulated and my capacity to help also increased by GOD's grace. The only rule we followed was that we always gave it to someone who could not do anything in return for us. Thus, it always was given and is being given to strangers and if household help maids' drivers are to be helped, we do it from our income and never from amount accumulated in the box. Now, I will share an experience that made me happy and thrilled. For about three years I did training, coaching and mentoring for Pen Plant of H&R Johnson tile company. From associates to top leadership, I conducted workshops and shared Success Mantras during which above experience of mine was also shared. I also could persuade the organization to give one post office shape box (one which children use for saving) to each participant. The cost of the box I insisted on being shared 50/50 by management and participant as it came to only Rs10/-. The box was given so that can use similar practice in their homes. After about a year when several associates (Team Members & Team Leaders) had attended the session, a few participants shared with me how they had utilized the above practice initiated in their home. All the participants of one section pooled all the amount of their box and went to hospital to give fruits to admitted patients. A group from another section purchased copies and pencil boxes and went and gifted children of a government school being run for tribal children. The practice continued for many years. When people understand and commit, they unite to do social work and that is the only way it can be done too.

When an individual tries to modify Society through his knowledge of society and talk alone, no change for the betterment can be made. However, **when an individual tries to modify Society by walking the talk through his own habits and behavior, it creates a Social Impact for larger good.** Each one of us is a part of Society and by synergy, which means the whole is bigger than the sum of the parts, we can do our bit as brought out above to impact Society.

The example of H&R Johnson exhibits this beautifully. Unfortunately, very few reflect and do something about it, going above their own ego, greed & self-interests.

Therefore, in effect, the room of Society, though is very much part of our life, it is hardly decorated. This is the reason the title of the chapter is not decorating the room of Society but just Cleaning the Room of Society. Even this will be done best when we join hands with others.

If only each one of us can do our duty, the world will become a better place to live.

Mother Teresa said it so well: **'If everyone would sweep their own doorstep, the whole world will be clean."**

Therefore, Success Mantra 8 is
Cleaning the Room of Society.

9

Decorating the

ROOM OF WORK

Success Mantra - 9
Decorating the **Room of Work**

The Room of Work, though mentioned last in the home of life, is the most important. Work gives meaning to life and gives you valuable learning, experiences and memories. It brings out the purpose for which you have come to earth and gives you the feeling of being worthy and useful. Sadly, many a time its value is realized more when you don't have it!

Jim Collins, in his book 'Built to Last', has brought out an important concept about the contribution of a human being while at work. He says one can be a time teller, a remarkable person who could look at the sun and stars at any time of the day or night and state the exact time and date. Like, today is March 1st and it is 2 am 36 minutes and 12 seconds. This person could be an amazing time teller and we could probably revere that person for the ability to tell time. But wouldn't that person be even more amazing if instead of telling the time, he built a clock that would tell the time forever, even after he was dead and gone?

Contribution at work has the power to make us immortal.

In my workshops, I ask participants to respond to these four questions:

- **Why one's work is important for himself?**

- **Why must one love his work?**

- **Why one's work is vital for one's future?**

- **Whom should one work for?**

Let us now deal with each:

Why one's work is important for himself?

One makes his living from the earnings at work. Thus, his and his family's needs such as food, clothing and shelter are met with these earnings. The education of his children, sustenance after retirement, when regular income is not there, health needs, travel and leisure, are all taken care of. Therefore, one's work is of vital importance for one's survival.

Why must one love his work?

Whatever one does, if it is not loved by him becomes a burden. Also, such work done out of compulsion never allows one to excel in that work. Couples who do not love each other find it challenging to be with each other even for a little time. With work, one invests so much of one's life, that if it is not to one's liking, life becomes stressful. Therefore, one must love his work, whatever it may be.

There is a beautiful saying, **"Do what you love and love what you do."** I say it differently, **"Keep loving what you are doing, till you get the opportunity to do what you love."** It is a fact that everyone is not lucky to start one's career with what one loves to do. In fact, in many cases one may not even be clear about the kind of work one really loves. However, when one keeps doing and learning any work, he gets the opportunity to switch over and choose what he loves to do.

In my own case, I loved learning and development and was lucky to get this opportunity in the early years of my career. I moved from teaching at the Engineering College where I had studied and was happy to join NTPC subsequently and loved my role in Training & Development there. However, I had to move to Human Resource Department on promotion and was in the role of Chief

HR at four power stations of NTPC and then as Vice President, HR in the private sector, loving my role as Human Resource Leader. Finally, after fourteen eventful years of eventful learning, I switched over to Coaching, Mentoring & Training in 2001 and am continuing in the same field and now work for myself. In hind sight, it is my stint in HR that helped me get many Organizational Development & Culture Building assignments in the last two decades.

Further, Marc Anthony has rightly said, **"If you do what you love, you will never work a day in your life."** I feel blessed to have been able to live this quote.

Why one's work is vital for one's future?

One usually retires from work when one is about 60 years of age, but lives for many more years. With longevity being the order of the day, one will continue to live for another 20 to 30 years. Until and unless he has a business or is active and keeps earning, he must survive on the savings made when he was working and earning. Besides, in many cases, if the children have not settled, one must provide for them too. Cost of maintaining one's health also escalates during this period. All such needs are to be met and require cash flow, which happens from investments made while one is working. However, such investments are to be planned and made while at work. Therefore, one's work is vital for one's present and future.

Whom should one work for?

One starts to work usually around the age of 22 and retires around 62. Thus, one puts in 40 years of his life at work. If it is assumed that the active life span is 80 years, then one is investing almost half of his life at work. Also, the years from 22 to 62 are usually the most beautiful years of one's life, as before 22 there are tensions of education, choice of career and an uncertain future and after 62, keeping oneself healthy and engaged is equally challenging.

Further, on an average one puts in at least 8 hours a day at work. If one sleeps for 8 hours and is awake for 16 hours, then one is living half of his waking hours at the workplace.

Summarizing all this, we can say one invests almost half of his life, the most beautiful years of life and half the waking hours at work. Therefore, even if the boss is not so good, work is not what one loves, remuneration is perceived as inadequate, one has to still be happy at work, full of energy, enthusiasm, passion and other positive emotions, since one is investing his life at work. Having negative emotions at work under any circumstances will be an injustice to one's life itself and if one is indulging in it, how can one do justice to anything else in his life. Life is most valuable and is to be lived fully, even at work. Therefore, one does not have to work for someone else, for an organization or a country but one has to work for oneself.

"Choose a job you love, and you will never have to work a day in your life." This is exactly what made me come back to a training role after many years and I really do not feel I am working!

The next question one must ask oneself is what does work give to him?

One earns money from work, which helps to meet one's basic needs besides expenses on education, health, emergencies etc. Work gives a feeling of being of some value and an opportunity to learn and contribute. Work earns respect and a sense of self worth too.

What does one give at work?

One gives his labor to work hard and his thoughts to decide what to do and how to do it. In other words, he utilizes both his body and mind at work. My question is, "Why not give one's heart too?" If one gives his heart to work, he will love it. If one loves one's work, if one enjoys it, one is already a success. The work then is not a burden or the cause of stress, rather it becomes a joy and brings happiness.

Rightly said, **"Your work is going to fill a large part of your life and the only way to be truly satisfied is to do what you believe is great work.'**

I am sharing what I once read:

How to manage Stress?

If you want happiness for a day, go on a picnic,

If you want happiness for a week, go on a vacation,

If you want happiness for a month, go on a world tour,

If you want happiness for a year, inherit wealth,

If you want happiness for a lifetime, **Learn to love, what you are doing today, that will make your life & earn your living.**

To love what you do and feel that it matters – how could anything be more fun- Katherine Graham

Your energy becomes magnetic when you love what you do. When you are passionate about what you do, you become a positive role model. You do not have to speak about your work, your work speaks for itself. Even your physical and mental health improves.

I love what Martin Luther King said about loving one's work;

" if it falls to your lot to be a street sweeper, sweep streets like Michelangelo painted pictures, sweep streets like Beethoven composed music, sweep streets like Shakespeare wrote poetry. Sweep streets so well that all the host of heaven and earth will have to pause and say: Here lived a

great street sweeper who did his job well."

Whatever your life's work is, do it well - put your soul in your job.

A person should do his job so well that the living, the dead and the unborn could do it no better.

My own experience is that my team practiced it everywhere and motivated me also to practice, thereby creating history whether it was at NTPC Training & Development Institute, NTPC Unchahar or the transformational culture in a Textile Plant. Even my participants at Tribal Welfare Department, MP created history for first time in the country with the success story of building a 'Learn and Teach' culture in hostels for tribal students.

Therefore, Success Mantra 9 is

"Decorating the Room of Work."

10

Practicing & Applying
SUCCESS MANTRAS

Practicing & Applying
SUCCESS
MANTRAS
1
2
3
4
5
6
7
8
9

Success Mantra - 10
Practicing & Applying Success Mantras

One important attribute that I learned at the beginning of my career was that of taking ownership. Usually, the word ownership is associated with material possessions, I feel lucky that I realised right at the start of my career that it is my Life, and I must take ownership of it. In simple terms, I understood that my life is made of my choices and the actions I take, thereby I took full responsibility for the outcome, without blaming others for mistakes and failures. It helped me immensely as I could invest all my energies in finding solutions   instead of being part of a problem. When I was in leadership roles with organizations, it also helped me gain the trust of my team, who knew that if they fail, I will be there for them, to take responsibility for the failure and also help them find solutions. It was unusual too.

Success has many fathers, but failure is an orphan

- John F. Kennedy

When I started working for myself and shared the Success Mantras, I always told participants that if they try to apply these mantras and succeed, it is their success, however, if they fail, it will be my failure, as I could not make them understand the application clearly. It motivated them to try without blaming themselves or others for failures. This was right too as:

If the student hasn't learned, the teacher hasn't taught.

We have by now learned and understood the nine success mantras. When I initiated interactions in my workshops, I realized that the participants took a lot of interest in learning these and even collaborated these by their own experiences of life. However, I felt that they need to utilize these by practicing in their life to get benefitted in the long run and live a happier life. The workshop was extended to two days. They were asked to apply the success mantras back home in the evening after the workshop and share their experiences of the previous day on the second day at the beginning of workshop. This practice was introduced because,

Knowing is good, Learning is better.

But it is only using this knowledge & learning in life in action,

that

the knowledge & learning get a meaning.

The practice of learning back home and sharing with the group had two benefits; one that they themselves experienced the utility of learning and second everyone learned from each other's experience. Taking ownership of life, thereby of choices and actions by them was demonstrated in a small way during experience sharing. They also realized that they and they alone can change and transform their life.

"A man has to learn that he cannot command things, but that he can command himself; that he cannot coerce the wills of others, but that he can mould and master his own will: and things serve him who serves Truth; people seek guidance of him who is master of himself.".. *James Allen*

On my part I tried to do everything that could remind them of the learnings of the workshop. My books in Hindi were written also to supplement the learning back home after the workshop.

Posters were developed and given to them to act as a daily reminder. One such poster placed below

We all want to be happy,
for being happy, we have to make everyone happy,
for making everyone happy, we have to be happy.

Happiness is a daily decision We can not be happy in past, nor in future...
We have to be happy in the present.

We cannot choose the circumstances, but we can choose our response to these.

Hence, keeping myself happy is my responsibility!

Think Positive & Be Happy

All these was just to motivate them to keep practicing and gather positive experiences, which will further motivate them to experiment and gain new experiences. There was a positive impact as the feedback made me realize. Yet, knowing and understanding fully that life might draw them back to routine, day to day challenges might dishearten then and they may forget the application of mantras, I kept exploring ways to enhance the impact of workshop, in a way that the participant continues practicing the mantras for which the starting point was to remember the mantras. When Facebook and WhatsApp came into being, I utilized these to share positive and motivating thoughts to keep reminding them that they should continue on the path to self-development. I am happy that all these small initiatives did help and are still helping.

However, an awareness that finally made significant difference was a realization that came to me, while reflecting on my own life that I continued practicing those things in life which had the following three attributes:

- I believed that I could do it

- I committed to what I will do &

- I continued doing it.

Thus, the tables were formed:

- **I can do it**

  (**Can** is belief, the starting point of any new beginning)

- **I will do it**

  (**Will** exhibits commitment to one's own decision)

- **I will continue doing it**

  (**Will Continue** denotes continuity of a practice to convert it into a habit)

This insight led me to an effective way to remember, practice and utilize success mantras. While interacting about Success Mantra 1, the participants were asked how many of them have to get up in the morning. Many hands were raised. Then they were asked how many of them think we should get up happily in the morning and again many hands were raised. When I asked them to reflect on what they affirmed, they realized **'have to'** means getting up under compulsion and **'should'** is generally used as advice to others. We all agreed this was not the right way to start one's day. This took us to coining the above table and success mantra 1 was chanted as follows.

Success Mantra 1

I can wake up happily in the morning

I will wake up happily in the morning

I will continue waking up happily in the morning.

And to remember it easily it was termed as table of 2.

I can wake up happily in the morning	**2 x 1=2**
I will wake up happily in the morning	**2 x 2=4**
I will continue waking up happily in the morning	**2 x 3=6**

Thus, it became child's play to remember the mantra, practice it and make it a habit by chanting Can, Will and Will Continue.

It paved the way for coining other mantras on the same lines, which made it so easy to remember, practice and convert the Success Mantras into a habit after which remembering these happened automatically. Participants started their morning with the chanting of Happy Morning, which made their family members at home and colleagues at work also do the same. The positive energy generated helped them to move forward in the day meeting challenges of life more effectively. Being Energetic and Charged they became happier, and the movement became contagious, which further helped to sustain themselves on path.

In this way tables for other mantras were developed on similar lines as given below.

Success Mantra 2

I can be lively	**3 x 1=3**
I will be lively	**3 x 2=6**
I will continue being lively	**3 x 3=9**

Success Mantra 3

I can do value addition to be valuable	**4 x 1=4**
I will do value addition to be valuable	**4 x 2=8**
I will continue doing value addition to be valuable	**4 x 3=12**

Success Mantra 4

I can be happy and try to make others happy	**5 x 1=5**
I will be happy and try to make others happy	**5 x 2=10**
I will continue being happy and try to make others happy	**5 x 3=15**

Success Mantra 5

I can utilize the Law of Attraction in my life	**6 x 1=6**
I will utilize the Law of Attraction in my life	**6 x 2=12**
I will continue utilizing the Law of Attraction in my life	**6 x 3=18**

Success Mantra 6

I can Decorate my Room of Self	**7 x 1=7**
I will Decorate my Room of Self	**7 x 2=14**
I will continue Decorating my Room of Self	**7 x 3=21**

Success Mantra 7

I can Decorate my Room of Relationships	**8 x 1=8**
I will Decorate my Room of Relationships	**8 x 2-=16**
I will continue decorating my Room of Relationships	**8 x 3=24**

Success Mantra 8

I can clean my Room of Society	**9 x 1=9**
I will clean my Room of Society	**9 x 2=18**
I will continue cleaning my Room of Society	**9 x 3=27**

Success Mantra 9

I can Decorate my Room of Work	**10 x 1=10**
I will Decorate my Room of Work	**10 x 2=20**
I will continue Decorating my Room of Work	**10 x 3=30**

Success Mantra 10

I can practice and utilize Success Mantras
I will practice and utilize Success Mantras
I will continue practicing and utilizing Success Mantras.

Practicing by application of the mantra brought home the utility and thus one who did this did not need any external motivation and results and achievements became one's own source of motivation. The spiral effect amazed me, as I had never imagined that this journey could take such dimensions. I shared only those simple actions that helped me with my own journey of living happily, energetically, enthusiastically and passionately. Anything I wished for in last forty years was fulfilled. Through my workshops I got connected to thousands of lives. In all my assignments my teams excelled in achieving amazing results, initiating new practices and creating history with their initiatives. At places where I was engaged, whether in roles or later as facilitator, the institutionalization process took place.

The purpose of bringing out this book is also to help you utilize success mantras for successful living. But I am also clear that it will only happen if you practice these mantras by application.

Looking back, I find I have lived a happy, blissful, and fulfilling life. Today I feel fortunate to live an abundant life, a grateful life, where I have more than what I need in all aspects. I get overwhelmed when I realize everyone from frontline associates to the topmost, people in my lovely dwelling Serene County or in organizations which I am assisting, in markets, hospitals or even at Shirdi my place of devotion, people do everything to make me happy, in small and big things. Every moment I am in gratitude to

SAI Shirdi for his blessings, to my family members, who shower love, affection and care and my numerous participants, who even after many years are connected to me if not personally through WhatsApp and share their happiness with me.

All the Success Mantras are simple choices one can make to live a happier life. These choices helped me all my life and are helping those who are utilizing these in their life.

I love this quote by Les Brown:

"The graveyard is the richest place on earth, because it is here that you will find all the hopes and dreams that were never fulfilled, the books that were never written, the songs that were never sung, the inventions that were never shared, the cures that were never discovered, all because someone was too afraid to take that first step, keep with the problem, or determined to carry out their dream."

Let us resolve to work for making our dreams come true. I did and am confident you will too.

This makes our journey come to an end in the book, but I do believe it could be the starting point for you to start living a happier and fulfilled life. I assure you of my commitment to assist you at any time if you ask me for the same. We are now connected even if we have not met and I will be happy to help you live a beautiful life.

I wish you Happiness, Health and Success.

Author

S. Nand is a Life Coach, Youth Mentor, Organizational Development Facilitator and a Motivational Speaker, who shares   simple insights for happy living. He has passionately conducted interactive workshops for more than two decades for participants ranging from front line associates to top leadership teams. Organizations that have benefitted from these, comprise of private and public sector, government departments, educational and medical institutions, and independent groups. He has facilitated a happy, positive and performing culture in several organizations such as H&R Johnson, RAMCO SYSTEMS , NMDC etc.

Nand did his Engineering from NIT Allahabad in 1969 where he also served as Faculty after passing out. He then moved into Training at FCI and while working there acquired Business Management qualifications. This led to his role in Training and Development at NTPC Shaktinagar and he was instrumental in creating an Institute, which became the pride of the organization. He later took on lead HR functions at four projects of NTPC. His noteworthy contribution was initiating an attitudinal change at Unchahar, a power station taken over by NTPC from the UP State Government. This turnaround is mentioned by none other than Late Dr APJ Abdul Kalam in his book India 2020. Finally, he moved to the private sector as Vice President (HR) and was successful in creating a distinctly different and positive work culture at the Textile Plant at Indore.

In 2001, Nand started working for himself and has touched more than two lakh lives in the last two decades through his 'Success in Life' workshops. There are innumerable stories of his participants living a happier life, building better relationships and working positively at the workplace. Presently he is assisting Jindal Power, Chhattisgarh with interventions to ensure a happier, positive and performing human resource.

Editor

Padmini B Patell is a committed social entrepreneur, passionate writer and an effective home maker . With Post Graduation Diplomas in Travel & Tourism, NGO Management & Social Entrepreneurship she contributed to Hindu's Metro Plus and Young World on subjects ranging from Culture, Heritage, Holistic living to Environment issues and Social Initiatives. She champions the cause of Nature Conservation in general and has a deep connect with rocks in particular and is presently Joint Secretary, Society to Save Rocks. Padmini started Mitravaan – Centre for Holistic Awareness, Secunderabad in 2014 which promotes the study of Vedanta and encourages conscious living for a peaceful planet.

Designer

Mr. Shanker pulgam skilled professional with more than 20 years of experience, web design, book publishing, designing, artwork and editing. He is fully committed whatever the projects he undertakes and takes responsibility of his role from start to finish.

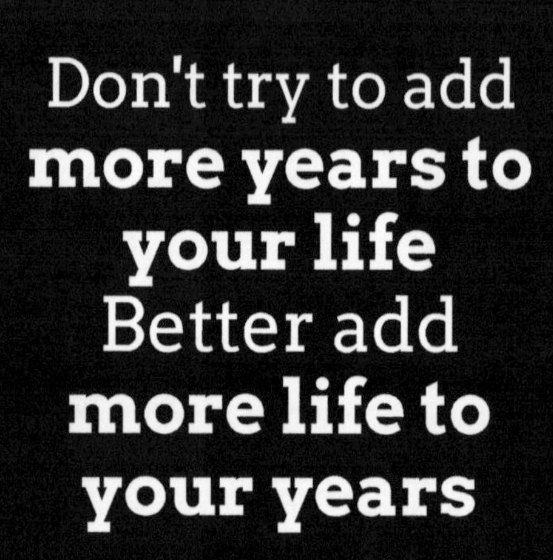

Don't try to add
more years to
your life
Better add
more life to
your years

Blaise Pascal